The Communal Desk
A Literary Lapse Chapbook

featuring the flash fiction of

John Cowan
Krys Douglas
Mary Ellen King
Gail A. Laursen
Laura Salamy
Tevia Wall
Gretchen Wilsenach
Kerry-lyn Witherspoon

InkSpotter Publishing

PUBLISHED BY INKSPOTTER PUBLISHING
163 Main Avenue, Halifax, Nova Scotia, Canada B3M 1B3
http://inkspotter.com/

Printed and bound in the United States of America by CreateSpace

Acknowledgements

The stories contained herein grew out of the camaraderie of the Literary Lapse mailing list, currently hosted at YahooGroups. To learn more about the group and about how to join, please go to http://ca.groups.yahoo.com/group/Literary_Lapse/

"Paternity's Nature" was a runner-up in the WOW Women on Writing Summer 2008 Flash Fiction Contest.

ON THE COVER

Inktiques
1905 20th Ave on Hwy 2 North
PO Box 301
Nanton , Alberta, Canada T0L 1R0
Phone: (403) 646-0008
Cellular: (403) 360-8226
E-Mail: shop@inktiques.com

Photo by Gail A. Laursen
Design by Betty Dobson

ALSO AVAILABLE FROM INKSPOTTER PUBLISHING

Backless, Strapless & Slit to the Throat
A Boy Named Wish
Collywobblers
Family Lines
Holiday Writes
Paper Wings

http://inkspotter.com/bookstore

AND COMING SOON

Breaking Free
Wait a Minute, I Have to Take Off My Bra
Writing the Bottom Line

http://inkspotter.com/publications/books

The Letter

John Cowan

"Pickin' it up here, boss."

"Pick it up, boy."

I picked up my grass sling and took off at a slow, shuffling trot. That was as fast as the shackles and chains would allow me to go. (For those of you who don't know, a grass sling had a long handle like a hoe or shovel. The top half was usually wrapped with electrical tape, for gripping with sweaty hands. At the business end was a blade about three inches wide and a foot and a half to two feet long. That was attached to the handle with two bent strips of steel and bolted in place. The blade was serrated on one side and fairly sharp. You swung the blade over your right shoulder, like swinging a golf club, then brought it down through the grass and up over your left shoulder.) The engine that ran that lawn-mowing machine was an employee of the State of Louisiana: me, Harley LeFlem. For this, the State of Louisiana gave me twelve cents an hour, three squares, and a cot.

The day the letter came we were cutting grass near Tunica. Me and a gang from Angola were at it for three or four hours in the blazing sun. Temperature was at least a hundred, not a cloud in the sky or a breeze of any kind. You couldn't see more than a few hundred feet in any direction for the heat shimmers. Every breath of that hot air was laced with dust, knats, and grass clippings.

"Gettin' a drink here, boss."

"Get a drink, boy. Make it quick. We gotta lotta grass to cut today."

I hustled over to the truck, where Toby Ross handed me a cup of cold water. He even got a little chunk of ice in it, big enough I could hold it in my mouth a little while. I just turned the cup up to my mouth when I saw the black shape coming through the heat shimmers rising off the blacktop. When it got close enough, I could see it was the prison chaplain's car.

"Hurry up there, boy!"

"Yes sir, boss. Yes sir. Hurryin' up here, boss. Thank you, boss." I shuffled back to the roadside and the grass. I just picked up my sling when the chaplain's car rolled past us and stopped. The boss nudged his horse over to the car. He spoke with the driver then raised up and called, "LeFlem!"

"Yes sir, boss. I'm here, boss."

"Front and centre, boy."

"Yes sir, boss."

I was planted near Mt. Airy, Saint John the Baptist Parish, Louisiana. My mother was a seamstress and worked in a little tailor shop in Mt. Airy. Late in 1926, a gambling man stopped in the shop to get some pants repaired. Late that night, after convincing my mother that she was the most beautiful woman he ever met and that it truly was love at first sight, Gerald LeFlem slipped out of town. The only thing he left behind was me. I was born Harold Broussard Guidry LeFlem in New Orleans at 12:03 A.M., July 4, 1927.

In order to save her family the embarrassment, my mother took me and her sewing needles and went to live in the big city. Problem was there wasn't a tailor in New Orleans who needed a pregnant, hick town seamstress. Momma did finally find work, though: seamstress in a home for girls called "The Rising Sun." The position paid well, had really good benefits and a steady stream of male customers, and allowed us a good living.

I was nine before I realized I was being raised in a whorehouse. I was eleven before I knew what that meant. I was fifteen when Lily Ann, a blonde from Virginia, explained what it really meant. When Momma caught us, two nights later, she slapped me and stuck Lily Ann in the breast with a sewing needle.

By the time I was seventeen, I was in and out of juvenile court several times. It wasn't hard to fall in with the wrong crowd when you were raised by whores. It didn't take me long to figure out that sewing wasn't the only thing Momma did there.

At nineteen, I got involved in loan sharking. I was hired by a shark as a collector and got a healthy commission on every loan balance I closed. One night, I cornered a mark in an alley and demanded he pay up. I really didn't think he'd talk back to my .38, but he was drunk. He attacked me with a machete, and I shot him in the head. Unfortunately, by the time the police arrived, his machete disappeared, but I was still holding my .38. They arrested me, took me to jail, and charged me with second-degree murder. I was tried, convicted, and sentenced to life at Angola, which is how I came to be cutting grass on the side of the road that day.

The last time I saw my momma was the day they put me on the train for Angola. She didn't come to any of my trial or sentencing. She didn't return my calls and never responded to my letters. I was standing on the platform when the train pulled in. I was handcuffed, shackled, and chained hands to feet, and they wouldn't let me sit down. I hurt all over from the beatings I received. My stomach hurt so bad I couldn't eat, and I was so hungry...then, as I started to step onto the train, I took one last look around, and there she was. Momma. She was just standing there, about ten feet away. There were tears running down her face, and she was smiling at me. Suddenly, I wasn't hungry, and my pain disappeared.

"Get moving." Someone shoved me from behind.

I stumbled over my chains and fell headlong into the prison car. "Please," I pleaded, "please, help me up." The guards grabbed the chain running down my back, jerked me up, almost dislocating both shoulders, and stood me by the only window in the car.

As the train started moving I looked out and saw her.

She smiled and waved and said, "I love you, my son." She followed as far as she could and waved till I was out of sight.

The walkin' boss took off my shackles then said, "Get in the car, boy."

I climbed into the back seat. It was so cool in there. I never saw a car with air-conditioning before. The chaplain was in the back seat with me. Once I was in, the walkin' boss got in the front by the driver.

The chaplain had an envelope in his hand and a sombre look on

3

his face. He held the envelope out to me and said, "This came for you, son."

The envelope was already unsealed, no doubt by the prison censor. I didn't want to, but I opened it and looked inside. I took out the single sheet of paper and read the official looking letterhead:

Office of the Medical Examiner
City of New Orleans, Louisiana

Slowly, I unfolded the crisp, white sheet of paper then read:

We regret to inform you that your mother, Rose Idella Breaux, passed away in her sleep from an apparent heart attack. Her death was quick and relatively painless. She was clutching several letters from you, and, as she held them so tightly, it was decided to bury them with her. Interment will be tomorrow in her hometown of Mt. Airy.

By the date on the letter, I knew the burial was two days ago. I looked at the chaplain as the first tear I shed in many, many years slid down my cheek. "Thank you for bringing this to me."

"You go on back to the house with the chaplain. You got the rest of the day off," the walkin' boss said.

I thought about it for a minute then said, "If it's all the same to you, boss, I'd rather stay and finish the day. It's a good day to work." I stepped out of the car, looked up to a sky as blue as Rose Idella's eyes, and thought, *Out here, Momma can see me and see what a good boy I've become.*

John Cowan is a sixty-year-old RN who lives in north-east Florida with his wife of thirty-five years, Robin, their daughter Kelly, son John, Jr., and grandson Michael.

Night Life of a Nymph

Krys Douglas

Music blared through the doors leading from the garden into the house. The sheer curtains billowed outward with the sound of laughter, clinking glasses, and the Charleston. Julie, tired of the noisy chatter and champagne, escaped to the garden and now leaned on a balustrade separating the lawn from a flagstone area, in the centre of which was a large fountain. Flare and sputter from torches on each side of the short stair leading to the flagstones cast more shadow than light.

"You must be more bored than I am," she said to the statue that stood in the fountain. She fingered trumpet beads that adorned her gown. "All you do is pour water into that pool. All I do is go to these silly parties."

"It's not so bad."

Julie straightened, startled. "Who said that?" She scanned the area as best she could. Torchlight revealed nothing.

"I did."

Julie turned toward the voice and looked directly into the eyes of the statue. The eyes looked directly back into hers.

"Y...you can't talk!"

"Whatever do you mean? Of course I can. I am," the statue said.

Julie looked at the statue more carefully. It was the typical Grecian-style nymph: flowing robes, hair up-swept in bands of ribbon, dignified and graceful, pouring water from an ewer.

"Of course," the statue continued, "I would like to put this blasted water pot down for a while. I've got a crick in my neck. Would you mind?"

"Mind?" Julie's discombobulated mind tried to make sense of this turn of events.

"Mind helping me get down from here for a few minutes."

"Ah...no. How would I do that?"

"Come over here and balance this thing when I step off the pedestal."

Julie went quickly down the few steps to the fountain area and, ignoring her satin high heels and party dress, stepped into the pool. As she raised her arms, the draped silk fell back to reveal her tanned arms. She supported the ewer as the nymph put a hand on Julie's shoulder and stepped into the pool. They both moved to the fountain's edge and sat on the broad rim.

"Oh, thank you." The nymph allowed the ewer to rest in the water. "I know you. You often come here to play that game." She lifted her chin in the direction of the tennis courts.

"Yes, I do. I'm sorry I've never paid attention to you before."

"Few ever do. These people throw parties that would make Zeus and Hera envious. Yet in the plethora of guests, not many even notice my existence." She spoke cheerfully enough, without rancour.

"How can you stand it?" Julie asked.

"Ever since people stopped believing in the Olympian gods, we take whatever jobs we can. At least this way people are still aware of us. It beats oblivion." She became thoughtful. "Still, there are things I miss. Strawberries!" She daintily licked her lips. "I do miss strawberries."

"I could get you some. Although I think all those at the house are dipped in chocolate." Julie rose to return to the house.

"Oh, no!" The nymph reached out and, taking her hand, pulled Julie back down. "Don't leave! As soon as you do, I have to get back up there! Anyway, chocolate is rather esoteric for my taste. We never had it at home."

"All right. I'll stay."

"Only one other person's talked with me in the last two years. He was at one of these parties, too. Now what was his name?" A small frown creased her forehead. "I remember! Johnny McKenzie."

"Johnny! Why, I came with him tonight!" Julie thought about the twinkle in Johnny's dark blue eyes, as if he knew something no one else did.

"He's a nice boy." The nymph looked at Julie knowingly. "You could do worse. Life would never be boring with him!"

Julie was about to agree when a pleasant male voice called her name from the grassy area above.

"Julie? Oh, there you are!" Johnny McKenzie came down the steps. "I see you two have met." His eyes fairly danced. "I hate to break this up, but it's started to rain."

Julie became aware of the light drizzle.

"You'd better go in," the nymph said. "Unlike me, you can catch cold." She smiled at the couple. "But I hope you will come to visit again."

"We will," Julie and Johnny said in unison.

"And we'll bring strawberries next time!" Julie cried as she and Johnny ran for the house.

Krys Douglas recently retired from teaching an eclectic variety of subjects (humanities, American history, religion, theatre, cultural studies...and English—when they got down on their knees and begged) at a community college in Albuquerque. She's had an equally eclectic variety of jobs (sales, receptionist, draftsman, editor, teacher, set designer, magician's assistant, and tutor). She won a prize in fifth grade for a poem and has been writing ever since. She's had many publications in non-fiction, mostly academic areas, and several publications of short stories and poetry.

Memory Foam

Mary Ellen King

My grand-kid comes home from school and hands me a note about a lice outbreak. I check out the Kwell at the pharmacy. It's expensive, so I go to my hairdresser.

I say cut it off.

She says how short?

I say shave it.

Everyone says the bald head brings out my eyes, but, after a few days, Bernie says I have a five-o'clock shadow and it gives him a rash in bed. Bernie needs to get a life, and I need a new mattress.

I watch the guy wearing a turban and full beard balance the Bob-O-Pedic memory foam across his shoulders and carry it into the house. I suspect the delivery guy is a mid-eastern terrorist. I'll ask Bernie to check for hidden explosives later. Bernie sits all day in the recliner, a can of beer in hand, smoking and wearing a muscle shirt, without the muscle. I look at Bernie and see a disappointment. After forty-three years of marriage, he ought to make something of himself. Still, he knows about explosives.

I start tidying the bedroom closet and find old letters stored in a See's candy box.

Dear Mom,

I'm finally in London. Had to talk my way into the country. The immigration officer wouldn't let me in at first.

How long you staying?

About three years.

I'll give you three weeks.

I'm here to work.

You can't.

Yes, I can.

No, you can't.

Honest, I can type and file.

That's how I found out there aren't enough jobs for the people already living in England. He let me in when I promised to get a job nobody else wanted. Now I'm a waste management engineer.

Love, Millie

I read the next letter in the pile:

Dear Mom,

I clean bathrooms in the wards of the maternity hospital and sluice the babies' dirty nappies. I live in the staff quarters. One day, Sister Blackburn walks in without knocking, and I'm standing there naked as a newborn Nelly. Sister looks me over. She smiles and leaves. Now what do you think that was all about?

On a day off from mopping up baby crap, I meet my soul mate in the underground at Marble Arch: Reggie, the Busker Boy, beating drum with his foot pedal, humming harmonica, open guitar case. He's famous now. If I only played things right...

Reggie is nice, but he wants me to sleep with him.

He says he wants to teach me more than playing guitar.

I say I'm not that kind of girl but guitar is fine.

He says here's five quid for a taxi.

Life goes on. I have a good job sterilizing my square foot of the world's environment; and I have a friend. Standing in the sluice room, rinsing human excrement off the bed sheets, I tell Maggie all about my love affair with Reggie.

I ask would she do that without being married?

She says yes.

I start seeing Bernie when Maggie and I meet him and Tall Charlie at Wimpy's. Charlie fancies me, but his nose is too big for my taste. Maggie doesn't seem to mind Charlie's big nose. It's a sign, she says.

Dear Mom,

Sister Blackburn is tight with a group of nurses who never mix with us. They can do as they like... as long as they don't bother me.

It's 2:30 in the morning and the wall phone outside my room wakes me up. It's Sister Blackburn.

Miss Millie, you are needed on the private ward immediately.

You must have the wrong person, I'm not a nurse.

You are needed for a cleanup, my dear.

Okay.

You must say 'Yes Sister, right away Sister.' You are not in America.

Okay.

I finish mopping up the blood and pus from a patient's burst abscess, wash the slime and goop off my hands, and consider a suggestion that cleanup people wear gloves. I hear footsteps come into the room and stop behind me.

I want you, Millie, Sister Blackburn whispers. She gives my right buttock a soft squeeze, and I spin instinctively. My suds-and-pus-dripping arm knocks Sister Blackburn to the floor.

Oops!

In the morning, Matron calls me to her office and tells me that my work isn't up to standard. Pull up your socks, Millie, she tells me.

Dear Mom,

Maggie and I moved to a one-room bed-sitter with a kitchenette and a privacy screen between our beds. Maggie likes to party. She says she'll settle one day and wants a baby boy to make up for a little brother who drowned in a YMCA swimming pool.

Maggie asks me to go out tonight.

I ask for how long.

Until midnight.

The fog is unbelievable. Its green murk gives new meaning to pea soup. The Queen says the prime minister ought to do something about the weather. The prime minister says Parliament should pass a law. The House of Lords says it's up to the House of Commons. The House of Commons says it's not a problem.

In the morning, I need a sanitary pad. Maggie says I can have her box; she didn't need them. And the newspaper reports that Parliament should pass a clean air act after the smog last night.

Dear Mom,

Have you ever heard of Guy Fawkes Day? Three hundred years ago, on November 5th, this fellow tries to blow up the Houses of Parliament, and now kids pull a stuffed dummy around in a wagon, begging 'A Penny for the Guy.' They buy candy with the money while the parents light bonfires in their back yards and shoot off firecrackers.

I remember Bernie telling me about the day he blew up the Franciscan Friars chapel. At the boarding school, Bernie said he'd raid the storage depot at the nearby Royal Air Force base, collecting blasting caps and chemicals. At five in the morning of November 5th, while the friars were singing in the chapel, a number of explosions detonated, shaking the eaves and rafters, making the poor friars run for their lives.

Bernie is so smart. Imagine knowing how to mix chemicals to make bombs.

Dear Mom,

Bernie works in the laundry, and he sorts out the dirty linens that I sluice upstairs. He says it's our special connection. Isn't that dreamy? We meet at the pub after work every day. The hospital would fire us if they knew we were fraternizing. Bernie takes me to dinner at Wimpy's. He's so romantic.

Maggie gains a few pounds, and I tell her to go on a diet. We work together collecting hampers of dirty sheets and hospital gowns from the wards. I'll pull them out, and she'll rinse off the crap. Sometimes, she runs to the bathroom and vomits, so we'll

11

trade and I'll sluice the crappola. One day, Sister Blackburn stands at the door watching us work. With arms folded, her button eyes follow Maggie's every move.

One morning, Maggie doesn't come to work. I go to the flat to see if she is sick. She comes out with a suitcase and with Reggie the Busker Boy's arm around her waist as he walks her down the steps. They don't see me, and they climb into a cab and drive away.

After I spend my fury calling Maggie and Reggie every damn name I can think of, Bernie kisses me and dries my tears with his handkerchief. I still have that handkerchief in one of my memory boxes.

Dearest Mom,

They found my friend, Maggie, lying in a back alley in Soho. The newspaper said she had a botched abortion. At the autopsy, they found what they called a 'product of conception.' It was a tiny baby boy.

After four years of courting, I marry Bernie. The matron finds out I'm pregnant, and I'm given my cards—which, in plain English, means I'm fired. Another two babies, and Bernie decides we should go to America and move in with my mom. He hasn't enough time from working the hospital job, pumping gas at night, and selling fireworks on Saturdays to work a fourth job.

Dear Mom,

We'll be home soon. The London newspapers just broke a story about Sister Blackburn. She was running an escort service, hiring out young nurses as call girls. Lots of ministers of Parliament have been caught with their pants down, and they are still finding connections with the royal family, it's said. Tell you more when we arrive.

I better put these old letters away and start supper. I hear Bernie coming upstairs. The new mattress the terrorist delivered today sure will feel good tonight. I'm looking forward to the fireworks, even if Bernie says there aren't any bombs hidden in the memory foam. How could I forget why I married him in the first place? Bernie's a keeper. And he sure knows his explosives.

He says hi honey, I'm hungry, what's for dinner?

I say bangers 'n mash, your favourite.

Mary Ellen King has a dream to write a novel. She grew up listening to her grandmother's fascinating stories of life in England, stories that inspired the creation of characters for her own short stories when she starting writing in the seventh grade. Mary Ellen studied and worked as a nurse in England while contributing articles to the Benedictine Abby Press in Ealing. Returning to the U.S, she freelanced articles and human interest stories in local publications. Her short story "Leaving Sherwood Forrest" was published in *The Rhode Island Writers' Circle Anthology 2008*. When not quilting or practicing her singing exercises, she can be found gazing at her unfinished novel sitting good-naturedly on a shelf at home in Woonsocket, Rhode Island, where she currently resides.

Careful What You Wish For

Gail A. Laursen

Prisca checked the mirror and adjusted her skirt. Then, pulling her lustrous black tresses free of her jacket, she smiled at the reflection. Beauty, longed for as a gawky child, became a wish granted. *Not bad for a gal my age!*

In the driveway, a horn honked. Grabbing her handbag from the chair, Prisca hurried out the door of her attic suite and down the stairs.

Carmen's Honda was parked close, spluttering and coughing. As Carmen threw open the side door for her and Prisca dropped into her seat, Kathy and Paul chimed "Hi Prissy!" from the back seat.

"Hi guys!" She barely shut the door, and the car was in reverse.

Braking hard at the street, Carmen grinned contritely. "Sorry. We're late."

Prisca looked back, and Kathy's shell-shocked gaze met hers. "Let's just get there, okay?"

The engine revved, and the vehicle lunged into the street, transmission screaming. A swift clutch change, and, after a few lurches, they sped off down the block.

The drive downtown continued at the same harrowing pace. Horns blared. Fingers were raised. *My, aren't we popular!* Prisca smiled at the absurdity.

Then Carmen ran the red light. The last thing Prisca saw was the horrified face of the bus driver as he careened towards them.

Pain, intense and all-encompassing, woke her. As she opened her eyes to slits, the light pierced her skull like a dagger. She shut them, breathing away the pain. Becoming conscious of the weighty restraint lying across her chest, she struggled to shrug it off, but shock waves of pain claimed her. Something warm gushed down her side. *Breathe!* Eyes still closed, she focussed on each intake and exhalation of air until

14

a viscous din of voices drew nearer. She lay still.

A cool hand took her wrist, fingers pressing firmly.

"I tell you, it's not possible!" a thin male voice near her feet protested.

The surface Prisca was bound to suddenly lifted and snapped to an abrupt stop, producing crushing pain along her side. More rolling and jostling before, finally, she was lurched to a final stop.

"I've seen stranger things," a hushed feminine voice near Prisca's head responded.

Prisca swayed then a door slammed.

"Yeah, but those other three...and it was her side mashed in, too!" Another door slammed. "Did you see it? Now that's a compact!"

"Dammit Frank! Shhhh..."

A siren whooped to life, drowning their conversation. Prisca felt hurried hands upon her, heard the rustle and clatter of medical care, but was soon lulled by the hypnotic sway and drone. Mentally, she shook herself. *Be ready!* The sensation, though, was always so blissful. Another mental slap. *Stay awake! This is no time for stasis!*

But revivification would not wait. It was dark when she regained consciousness.

"We'll move her immediately, Lieutenant." Papers shuffled beyond the doorway.

"Thank you, Doctor."

Prisca strained to hear their conversation.

"The other three?"

"Dead on impact."

No! Prisca's heart clenched with grief.

The lieutenant said something, the words "top secret" rising from the murmur. A chill ran through her. Memories of darker days loomed.

"I'll have a guard posted within the hour." This was followed quickly by more paper shuffling, a click, and the sound of several footsteps heading away.

Time to leave!

An hour later, she limped out the east door, wearing hospital staffer Flora MacDonald's clothes, a scarf wrapped closely about her battered face to evade the cameras' eyes. Flora's coat pocket contained change enough for bus fare, and, within twenty minutes, Prisca was approaching Shady Elms Crematory Mausoleum.

She advanced cautiously, glancing furtively about before staggering inside, where, in minutes, she pried open her niche. From its depths, she withdrew a tightly sealed plastic bag and tore it open. The new passport and an envelope filled with various currencies were stuffed quickly into coat pockets. Then she carefully removed the last item, a small wooden chest; she stared at it, tempted to leave it there. She couldn't bring herself to do it, though. Instead, she rewrapped it, tucked it inside her coat, and left.

The next afternoon, she boarded the *Atlantic Princess* as Tasia Ambrose, shrouded in a scarf and dark glasses. She posted a "Do Not Disturb" sign on her cabin door and took to bed. Despite her restorative needs, it was just too unbearable to watch yet another beloved country slowly recede into her past.

As she swiped away tears, the chest suddenly loomed into view from its place on her nightstand. She sat up, unable to resist its draw, and took it onto her lap. The ebony was well burnished now, its intricately carved surfaces smoothed by the ages. Prisca gently fingered the single Palm Branch hieroglyphic blazoned in gold across its centre. As she opened its lid, the smells of her childhood wafted up, soothing her. She gazed down at the golden Ankh-shaped hand mirror, its polished silver face turned down. Its back was decorated with two familiar symbols. Around its outer edge the Shen symbol, inlaid in green malachite, with its base riding the cross line of the Ankh. It was a sinister reminder of the mirror's power. In its centre, the Eye of Thoth, inlaid with jet, stared back mockingly.

Prisca reached in, took hold of the handle, the gold warm to her touch, and raised it. Turning it slowly, she peered into its face and that of the decrepit crone who returned her gaze. "If only leaving didn't hurt so!" She and the crone cried out in unison.

The mirror thrummed in her hands. "Will that be your third wish, Meskhenet?"

Gail A. Laursen, a graduate of Northwest Community College, returned to her first love, writing, after thirteen years in corporate accounting. Gail successfully completed two accredited correspondence writing courses and, in the interim, enjoyed brief experience as staff reporter for *The Valley Times* before moving from Drumheller, Alberta. A self-proclaimed gypsy, Gail has lived in various communities throughout British Columbia, Alberta, and Manitoba and is currently living in Cache Creek, BC, where she plans to continue work on her historical-fiction novel and her bi-weekly blog, *Thriving On Thrift*. Gail's femme fatale short story "Awaiting IIer" was published in InkSpotter Publishing's anthology *Backless, Strapless & Slit to the Throat*. As one of a team of moderators for a popular on-line writer's group, Gail derives great pleasure in contact with a global community of writers, editors, and publishers. In her spare time, Gail engages in diverse reading interests; outdoor adventures (fishing, bicycling, hiking, and rock-hounding); nature and landscape photography; sewing; and cooking up assorted Foodie delights.

Paternity's Nature

Laura Salamy

I blame my wife for the current domestic upheaval. I didn't even want to go that route, purchasing anonymous sperm. "Let's adopt from China," I said. "Girls go begging there."

"No," she maintained. "Our child has to be at least partly ours. Genetically, I mean."

"Why?"

She couldn't articulate a response but was more passionate about the matter. I acquiesced.

Her gynaecologist provided a catalogue. We studied the obvious. Education. Skin, eye, and hair colour. We delved into ethnicity, trying to match to our own disparate northern European and eastern Mediterranean roots. Requisite jokes were made regarding the costs of something most any guy would give away.

I signed up front—before conception—that I would be the father of record, the one named on the birth certificate rather than Donor Number 1503.

And I was: father to a beautiful, albeit loud and slightly cone-headed, fuzzy red-haired girl born late one August evening. Julia may be the one who insisted on how we became parents, but that summer night, my ambivalence was forgotten, and I fell in love with my...our own.

"Of course, we'll tell her about the genetic father," Julia insisted. "But only when she's ready."

And we did. After "Where do babies come from?" ("Mommy's tummy," of course) became "How does Daddy's seed get in there?" we knew it was time. No fuss was made, and Daddy's little girl was cool with her less than usual origins. Until last week, that was. Last week, Christina turned sixteen.

"I'd like to learn more about my real father." This was followed by a bit of sensitivity: "I mean my birth father, Dad."

"Just what are you interested in?"

"Like, well, I'm not exactly sure." She couldn't articulate what she was after, just that she needed to know.

"Why don't you start with this folder? Mom kept all the important papers in it." By "important papers," I mostly meant the catalogue of semen donors and Number 1503's medical history.

We hadn't bothered to buy the expanded package: detailed college and potential career notes, an essay, a recording of his voice.

"Unnecessary," Julia had also insisted. "Plenty of women have children with men they've barely met. Who knows what's swimming around in anyone's family history? Besides, you're her father, the only one she'll ever know."

I couldn't—didn't—disagree.

But, sixteen years later, I am clearly not enough.

And yet, I'm all there is. Julia's gone since last summer. Ovarian cancer.

Per Christina's request, I recently logged on to the Cryobank's database. Donor Number 1503 wasn't listed as active anymore. After so many years, that wasn't unexpected. I bought the still available notes, essay, and voice but couldn't get an address, a phone number, or a relationship. Nothing, not even natural law, could require that.

I hope these things help Christina, that they give her something to grab onto. I wish I saw it coming years ago.

I should've seen it coming.

I am her father, after all.

Laura Salamy lives and writes in Massachusetts with her husband, a labour-intensive adolescent daughter, and two dogs with attitude. She's had stories and essays published in *Get Born* magazine, the Providence and Boston newspapers, and online. Rug hooking competes with writing and reading for her artistic attention, so she asks that you please contact her if you know a good yarn shop.

New Beginnings

Tevia Wall

Winter hovered greedily at the edges of fall this year.

The snow line on Five Peaks had already begun skirting down the slopes, lower than it had been the same time last year.

There was a lot of work to do before winter settled in for good. The apple cellar was finally full, but the sheep still had to be sheared and two of the horses re-shod. Jake brushed smooth circles across the body of his mare, and she whinnied in delight, expelling a puff of white steam from her nostrils.

Early morning rides had become a kind of balm for Jake after his father had abandoned the family five years ago.

Jake grabbed the saddle blanket his aunt Deborah gave to him just last night for his birthday. It was clean and bright and smelled too fresh. He knew he needed to break it in, to let Selia get used to it. His old blanket was still plenty useful, so it would be passed to one of his younger cousins. It lay there, draped across the railing, looking forlorn and betrayed, so unlike his joyful heart. He heaved the new one across Selia's back and tugged it up just below her withers. She pawed her front hoof on the ground, letting him know she was anxious to get moving. He patted her neck and murmured soft words into her velvet ear.

They stood together under the light cast by a single naked bulb hanging from the rafters. A chill wind swept angrily past the partially closed doors, nipping the warmth from his uncovered skin. Was it just last night that he stood here in the dark with Meg, pouring out his heart and intentions to her?

He had been bold in his declarations and hadn't been disappointed with her response.

He felt giddy now, remembering the warmth of her lips against his own, and he could almost feel phantom fingers where hers so recently intertwined with his. He shivered—and not entirely from the cold.

Jake tightened the cinch and flopped the stirrup over the side, pulling on it to ensure it was tight enough. He would check the saddle again after riding for a while. Selia still liked to fill her belly with air while he tightened things up. She shook her head, and, as Jake walked by, a few strands of her mane whipped him lightly across the face. He patted her nose then grabbed the bridle. She opened her mouth without much coaxing and allowed Jake to slip the bit quickly into place.

Jake loved the cheerful jangling from all the tack, but he especially loved the groan and squeak of leather as he heaved himself up into the saddle. He stood and stretched his legs in the stirrups. Selia didn't need the slight tug to the left to head for the stable door. He hugged his jacket close and left the relative warmth of the building. The ground crunched noisily underfoot, and their passage left inverted U-shaped marks in the white frost. Looking up, Jake watched the last of the straggling stars in the western sky slip off to bed as the first dim light of the sun spilled across the horizon. Long strands of pink and gold slowly unfurled on the bland pallet of sky.

His thoughts wandered back to Meg, to their embraces in the darkness of the barn last night. He was ready. Ready to start this next phase of life, and to have Meg by his side was more than he ever hoped for. Looking along the western edge of his property, he was convinced that he could give her the life she deserved. Jake knew his hard work and integrity gave him the upper hand in winning the approval of Meg's father, but it was Jake's kindness and loyalty that sealed Meg's heart to his.

A long stretch of open land lay ahead of him. He squeezed his legs and encouraged Selia into a gallop. Her gait changed swiftly as she responded to Jake's well-known touch and shot off, running like the wind. The landscape flew past him, and soon he was at the northernmost edge of his property. He reined in his horse. When Selia came to rest, he let the reins fall down her neck. She mouthed the frozen ground, looking for any scrap of grass she could find. Jake paused a moment, reflecting on the beauty that surrounded him. He humbly bowed his head, arms folded across his chest. He spoke to his God, thanking Him for the bounteous blessings he received. He pleaded with his maker for strength and guidance during this new chapter of life unfolding before him. He murmured a quiet "amen" and wiped away the small trail of tears that trickled down his cold cheeks.

A gust of wind caught the edge of Jake's jacket, sending icy fingers up his back. There were many chores to be done, and he was confident the day would go by swiftly. Already the frost on the ground was becoming patchy, giving up its hold on the earth to the scattered rays of sun shining through the clouds. He knew Meg would be waiting for him at the house that evening, just as she promised. The thought made his heart beat rapidly. She would soon be his wife. Together they would work the land side by side, creating the life and family that he always dreamed of.

Tevia Wall lives in Phoenix, Arizona, with her husband and three sons. Her computer is currently bogged down with many writing beginnings but not a lot of endings. She was brave enough to enter a flash fiction contest, and her piece received a second runner up spot, which created great joy in her heart and stoked the fire to keep on writing, despite her busy life. Her goal is to write something worthwhile and inspiring, if only for herself, and for it to actually get a proper conclusion.

No More Bets!

Gretchen Wilsenach

My dearest Alexandria,

This letter may come as a surprise to you. It may also shock you to know that, some time ago, I decided to become a whore! Oh, how I wish I could see your face right this second.

But let me not forget my manners. How are you, my darling sister? How was the trip down the Nile? I hope it was as resplendent as the brochures promised you it would be.

And let me immediately apologize for not having written sooner. Once you hear my tale, you will understand everything.

Remember about six months ago, I had this inclination to go gambling again? I was behaving myself for so long, and withdrawal symptoms suddenly attacked me like a vampire. I had to go. I left London one foggy evening and flew directly to Las Vegas, where shining, glittering lights and water fountains awaited me with abundance.

The ritual of booking into the extravagant hotel and the odour of the casino as I walked to my glamorous suite were intoxicating. I could hardly contain myself and almost ran to the nearest roulette table. But I did not (you will be delighted to know). I had to prepare for the night's amusement in my usual fashion. How I wish you were there!

Dressed, jewelled and perfumed, I walked the length of the casino, looking for the stage of my performance. I found the roulette table just off the main floor and slipped into an open chair. I took a sip of soda water and a deep breath and laid my first bet, a bit timidly, as always. My insides were doing the cha-cha, however!

I raked in chips and placed more bets, small amounts, not too many. Then, at the very instant I was beginning to feel the energy surge through me, I saw this Greek god come into the room. In fact, I was not sure if he was a Greek god or a Spanish matador or a

23

sheik from Arabia or what! He just had this presence that preceded him into the room, and, for some reason, I felt weak when he took a chair next to me. What if...?

Slowly, I took bigger chances...then bigger...and sure enough, the pile of chips started looking absurd in front of me. Almost embarrassingly so. I smiled apologetically.

Then that omnipresent man started fumbling. To my surprise, he turned to me and said, "I seem to have lost my wallet. This is a catastrophe and an embarrassment."

"Hmmm, yes," I wanted to say but did not. We have all heard that one before, have we not, Alexandria?

The man turned to me again and asked if there was ever the slightest possibility that I could help him out of his predicament. I was about to refuse, Alex, when I looked into his eyes, and it was at that moment that I became a whore.

"I believe an arrangement can be made," I whispered back. He told me how much he needed, and, without hesitation, I did the unthinkable. (I know you are going to be so mad at me now.) I swept all the chips in front of me across to him. After tipping the dealer very generously, of course! I smiled at everybody's surprise, including his, and left the table.

Father would have died on the spot, and poor Mother would have surely fainted had they known what their daughter had turned into.

I never expected to see or hear from him again. But you know what? That was almost the most fun thing I ever did.

I flew back to London the next day—my appetite well sated. But not before the concierge gave me an envelope. It was from *him*. Let me tell you what he wrote:

Your graciousness, your trust, your extreme sense of adventure are even more beguiling than your beauty. I will repay every chip with interest.

Yours,
Guatam Thapar Maurya
Rajah of Rajasthan

Alexandria, what would you have done? We both know that I never lose at roulette; it is one of those strange, unexplainable anomalies—to my advantage or detriment?

Months went by, and I never heard a word, as I expected.

Last July, we went down to the south of France, *en famille*, to Count Cheninoux's chateau, by now an annual visit. I do believe that you were also invited but refused. I forget why. Why?

Alexandria, my dear, you will never guess what happened next. Or maybe you will because you know me so well. The casino of Monte Carlo beckoned, and I had to go! So many years passed since my last visit there, so I assumed I would be safe. I do not frequent conquered casinos!

I was raking in chips happily when I felt the power leave me, like energy evaporating. When I looked up, who was standing there? You guessed! The Rajah of wherever. He smiled as if he just won a game. Maybe he thought it was Christmas again? Not tonight, I sang softly. Before I knew what was happening, he politely asked if I would be so kind as to dine with him. It was on the tip of my tongue to ask who was paying, but instead I bit my tongue.

You would have been proud of me.

Darling, I am rattling on, as is my way, but this letter is really to invite you to come visit us in India.

I ran away and married Guatam. The family went slightly berserk, but I was never happier in my life. You see, that night in Monte Carlo, Guatam offered me a ruby that took my breath away. My desire to gamble was suddenly replaced with the desire to wear his ring and look into his mesmerizing eyes for the rest of my life. His palace is paradise, and I love India. He wants me to be his very own whore forever. I cannot help but laugh again. Don't be shocked, sister dear. At our age, we should be so happy this can happen.

Your loving sister,
Mathilde

Gretchen Wilsenach found herself being a bit of an anomaly all her life. She was born in South Africa with a German name (her father loved the name Gretchen) then married a man with a German surname, Wilsenach (he too was far from being German). She started writing as child, making her own magazines with illustrations and text. After school, she did a few years at an art college but soon progressed from artist to wife and mother. She never gave up on writing, though. Decades later, she knows all about animation and advertising, television and radio production, and running a restaurant and a bed & breakfast. But nothing matches the satisfaction she gets from writing—an adventure she can pursue forever.

Bunduki's Lament

Kerry-lyn Witherspoon

Bunduki (n) (b –<u>oo</u> / n – d<u>oo</u> / kie) *Swahili*: firearm or rifle
Nyati *(n) (N-yah-tee) – Swahili: buffalo*
Mbogo *(n) (M-boh-<u>g</u>oh) – Swahili: enraged buffalo*
Simba *(n) (S-im-bah) – Swahili: lion*
Moran *(n) – Swahili: Warrior, as in Maasai Moran*
PH *– Professional Hunter, as in a hunting guide who leads groups of hunters*

Dear Reader – That you better understand my story, this is my lament—the story of my revenge.

A proud .450 Watts BRNO, of converted Eastern Bloc extraction, I have been the devoted hunting companion of my PH Mark Radloff for many, many years. I have loved him. Countless have been the buffalo we have shot together, many the elephant faced, lions rolled, leopards taken from the branches of trees. I have been faithful. Faithful!

Then he went and left me in the dark of a safe for a time whilst he made use of that other weapon, a showy girl. He left me. This is the story of my revenge, then—of the time he took me out for an airing and fired me like in the "old days" before his infidelity. I had to return the favour...

The sun is not yet behind the horizon. Reeds stand tall—pointed, male, arrogant—between Nyati and my love and me. His hand rests on me, idly stroking where it used to hold tight in the days long ago when he took me out more often than he does these days. I feel dry under his hand, my sights a little jaded, faded from lack of attention.

There were those days, something like this one, when we would be together all day, from the hour before the sun to the time when the sky seemed to melt into the earth in the evening. All day he would carry me tenderly, caressing me, carefully tending me. Minding my shine and my actions, he took better care of me then.

These days, I am passed over, in most part, for an ostentatious double model, and the knowledge hurts me even as he does not seem to notice the wound of his infidelity.

A week, maybe two weeks ago, perhaps in guilt, perhaps in fond memory and longing for a good hunt, he slid me out of my cover and lifted me to his shoulder. It was an easy action, born of long practice. Born out of the hours, the days we used to spend together. Days when he slid me across his chest and into his arms with a simple reverence. A week, maybe two, he took me out of the dark, gave me an airing. In his hands, resting against his shoulder, I wondered where that showy new love might be.

In what place in his tent does she lie?

Has she even been brought on this trip with us? Has he oiled her well, caressed her lately?

Or is *she* in the dark now, covered, in favour of me, his old love, his faithful love?

He thinks he can get away with forgetting me. He thinks he can leave me alone, lying forgotten in a corner whilst he tends his new girl. Slides her home, sights along her clean line, nestles her into his shoulder. He thinks this. As he holds me in his dry, familiar hands and pulls me into his shoulder, clasps me hard and gazes at my length and loveliness, he thinks he can forget me then, in whatever whim plays in him, take me out again and expect me to be grateful. Expect me to be forgiving. For a smart man, this hunter of mine clearly has no real understanding of the nature of jilted love, and it's a lesson he must learn.

The sun is not yet on the horizon, and the reeds stand tall before us. In a tree, a bird calls: a hoopoe, little harbinger of ill fortune. He calls, and, from another branch, his mate answers. Echoes of ill fortune. We have long to wait for things to be right. We wait until the sun begins to slip like a segment of orange down along the distant hills, into the waiting arms of the trees; ahead of us, lying here, the herd stamps and frets. Overhead, a Marshall eagle shrieks.

By late afternoon, we have not yet killed.

We must be very careful with that herd. They are grazing close to the shade. The only way we can get close is to slide in the dust and grass on our bellies, as silent as Chui, the leopard; just a single snap of a twig could make the whole herd raise dust. My love scoops a handful of the dust and grass and lets it run through his fingers to see which way the wind is blowing. It is almost right.

Earlier, we ran like cheetah to the other side of the buffalo herd until one of the men gave a sign that all were in place. It was then that he slung me across his shoulders and began his slide through the powdered earth towards the herd. I felt that bump along his body like an old ache.

It has been such a long time since he has taken me out into the African sun and slid, with me balanced on him, to a place from where he can cradle me, stare along my body and, slipping a finger into me, slowly coax a shot out of me.

We used to hunt together a great deal, my hunter and I. And then he went and found himself a new love and left me, sulking, in the dark.

And now, here in the late sun, waiting for the perfect chance, he expects me to be forgiving?

Long we all lie in the heat, with the cry of the Marshall eagle overhead and a treacherous little Loerie calling his warnings from the trees. The men with my hunter all lie low, waiting for the wind to be just right. Ahead, through the reeds, the herd shuffles and chews. Little shifts of wind blow at them, not enough to give us away but enough to keep them on edge. Long we wait for the killing time to be right, and long do I lie with my hunter as in the hunting days before he thought to usurp me with that flashy mistress. In muted voices, the men talk, and, from time to time, my hunter runs his hand along me as if to make sure I am still with him. Does he think these caresses, this attention, will make right my abandonment?

There is grass on the hill where we lie and scattered bushes, and there is also forestation down in the V of the small hills. I hear the men talking, saying how they must stop Nyati from making it down to the thicket if he starts to run. If he runs in there, we will lose him for sure in the Miombo forest, thick and green. White egrets follow in the footsteps of the buffalo, eating the insects that they unearth with each step of their hooves. From a far-off hill, Simba grunts—perhaps he, too, waits long for a kill and is growing edgy. We all wait in the heat of the afternoon, and none waits more anxiously than I for the perfect moment.

The trackers lie quietly, talking amongst themselves in voices scarcely above a whisper, and they ask one another riddles to pass the time. *What do the Moran resemble when they stand on one leg?* And another will answer, *The Euphorbia trees.* Yet another asks, *What are the two skins I possess, the one I lie upon and the one that covers me?* A moment of still passes before Chilemba, my love's favourite tracker, replies, *One is the earth and the other is the sky.* Small smiles play on all their faces in acknowledgement of his clever answer. We wait. We all wait in the heat for the killing moment to be right, for the big bull, for big Nyati to stand just right for his killing.

My hunter sleeps a little in the sun, but, even in his rest, he is aware of the sound of the wind in the branches or the distant trumpeting of an elephant; even in his sleep, his chest vibrates when Simba roars on the far hill, and he is alert to the restlessness of Nyati: the cantankerous, irritable stamp of his hooves and the shake of his huge boss. Even in his sleep, my hunter knows Nyati is preparing to run, and he wakens, primed, knowing the hunting moment is come.

Nyati turns to trot down the hill towards a clump of bushes, and my hunter tells the younger man with us to shoot. *Shoot now! Shoot now before Nyati gets too far. Once he is in that thicket, we will have a devil's job finding him again!* And the younger man levels his puny .375 and shoots, but the lesser calibre of his girl only wounds; it does not have the impressive stopping power that I, proud .450 Watts that I am, have.

Nyati roars, wounded but slightly and unsure what he hears, perhaps a tree falling, a branch snapping. The wind does not give us away so Nyati cannot know for sure what he hears, but he grows irritated by the small pain of his wound; he grows furious, and he rattles his brains around in his great head as he shakes his horns this way and that. My hunter, thinking to prove his love for me, like in those old days before the new love, before he left me alone for the allure of that brassy .500 double N.E., thinking to prove his love for me all over again, raises me to his shoulder as he lifts to his feet and begins to run after angry *Mbogo-who-was-Nyati.* The other men rise, too, seizing their guns and their shooting sticks and giving chase, but my hunter is still as swift as the cheetah and even more graceful as he runs ahead, raising me to his shoulder, holding me tightly in his hands, sighting along my body, drawing breath as he tucks his finger around my trigger and eases me into shot.

Ah! The precise killing moment for him! I have waited such a long time for this. For such a perfect moment.

His finger is slow—a slight loss of sensation from an old stabbing wound in the elbow of his shooting arm—as it slides into me.

He forgot all these months past how I laboured with him after that wounding, toiled to get that lazy finger working again; how we learned to work together using the other arm, the other shoulder, the other hand. Together, we achieved this so he could work with me using either of his hands efficiently.

But now, unfaithful creature that he is, he slides his slow finger into me and expects me to remember it all for him as I recoil, loud and furious, into him. *Mbogo-who-was-Nyati* doesn't even break his stride. Under my thunder, under my lamenting howl, I hear the crack of my hunter's finger against my trigger guard, and I smile.

My love tries to shoot again; he tries to slip that old finger into me again, but there is nothing there to slip with. The finger-bone is broken in two and curled up on itself, and there is no love and no forgiveness that will make it straight again.

As yet unclear why there is no response in his shooting finger, he tucks me under his arm; he is yet to register pain, and he runs still towards *Mbogo*. With his other hand, he pulls at his wounded finger, trying to hold it into place as he calls to the younger man to shoot again. This time, that lesser rifle does what is expected of her. *Mbogo* falls heavily, his rage and his breath whispering out. And as the men all cluster around his great fallen form, my hunter looks down and sees, for the first time, the extent of the damage wrought by me. And *then* he feels the agony, and I can only trust it matches that which I feel.

When the hour of dusk draws near, the sun disintegrates into the sky and dusts the earth with a film of gold, and I lie beside my hunter as he tries to sleep, doped against his pain, his snapped and swollen finger held straight with a twig torn from a tree and a tie of cloth. I lie beside him, smirking, for there is still some hunting to be done; his broken finger will swell even more, and it will ache against that twig till the tears fall.

And I? I will have taught my love a lesson not easily forgotten.

Not as easily as he forgot me.

He will have to suffer for three full days, waiting to get into a town at the end of this hunt before he can have attention for that finger, and he will find, in colossal pain, that he will not forget me again. I lie, couched warm, in my rightful place beside him. Perhaps now, considering the hunt, dead Nyati, and the shattered finger-bone of my hunter, perhaps I am a little more willing to be forgiving. Perhaps now, too, as he suffers, he will understand that I am not to be replaced with that strumpet again.

Kerry-lyn Witherspoon is a forty-five-year-old South African citizen currently residing in Tanzania, East Africa. She shares this life with the proverbial "bushboy" Mark (so called for his love of the African bush and her creatures) and two daughters: Piper-Moore, soon bound to Calgary, Canada, to study Developmental Psychology, and Cammy, who will also go to Calgary in two years to follow studies in Photographic Journalism. The family also includes a mad black dog called Meme (Swahili for electricity, the colour of which this dog is!), a small toilet-brush-on-legs hound called Harry, a skinny cat called Biltong Jones, and a huge beast of a cat called Mouse-the-Mostly-Brave.

Kerry-lyn has always written—it's a compulsion that she cannot escape. She has had a few poems published in a small book in South Africa and has won two awards for short stories. Beyond this, she has not published—something to do with not having sufficient courage...yet! Kerry-lyn has completed one full-length novel about life in Malawi and Tanzania, taking a harsh look at the stuff of Africa and grief and recovery.

She is currently working on another novel, with a more tongue-in-cheek approach to life in the African bush. This life involves endless rounds of mosquitoes, snakes in the rockery, insects that cause one to swell and itch, a singular lack of reliable power, electrical machinery that gives up the ghost from power surges that come howling down the lines outside the house, scant telephonic connection and lamentable shortages of the niceties of life—like couscous or raisins!

A psychologist by qualification, Kerry-lyn has worked in a myriad of jobs from counselling (of recalcitrant youth!) to journalism, Training and Development Manager for a cellular company, and restauranteur.

Now, here in the hot heart of Africa, she works as a design consultant for safari companies and, in whatever spare time she has, flying to places as diverse as South Africa one week, the Serengeti the next, and China the week after—all for work. In between flying and working and the dismal power outages, Kerry-lyn tries to keep sane by putting "herself" into words.